That One Spooky Night

Written by Dan Bar-el
Illustrated by David Huyck

Kids Can Press

ONE NIGHT ...

BUT NOT JUST ANY NIGHT ...

SOMETHING HAPPENED.

hiss

IT HAPPENED HERE ...

AND IT HAPPENED HERE.

IT HAPPENED HERE ...

AND HERE ...

AND HERE ...

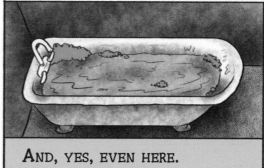

AND, YES, EVEN HERE.

SOME SAY IT WAS THE PLANETS' DOING.

SOME SAY IT WAS ALL JUST A BAD DREAM.

SOME SAY IT WAS AN EVIL WIZARD'S PLOT.

ACTUALLY, ONLY ONE SAID THAT.

BUT EVERYONE REMEMBERS ...

THAT ONE NIGHT ...

MANY STRANGE EVENTS REPORTED

OCTOBER

THAT ONE PARTICULAR NIGHT ...

THAT NIGHT LIKE NO OTHER ...

THAT ONE *SPOOKY NIGHT.*

OOOOOOH!
Look at **THAT!**

Don't worry, honey.
You'll get lots of
candy tonight.

10

GISELLE, SLOW DOWN!

CAN'T, MOM!

THIS BROOM ...

... IS TOO FAST!

WHAM

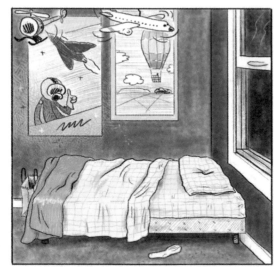

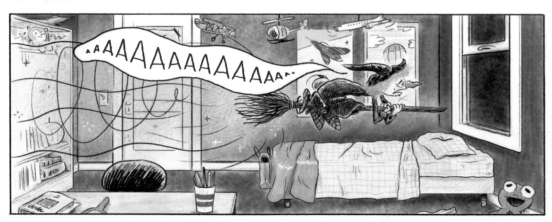

OUCH.

WHUMP!

There you are, Broomy. I had to walk all the way home.

Well, back to work.

yawn

A bit of frog legs.
A bit of bat wing.

A little snake venom.
A little llama spit.

And what's that?

Pepper.

Give it a
good stir,
Dearie.

Hop on,
Dearie.

Here you go, Count. Some nice warm soup won't bother your fang-ache.

Th-th-that's ...

Yes, Dearie, that's what you get when you don't brush your teeth.

WOW AND DOUBLE WOW.

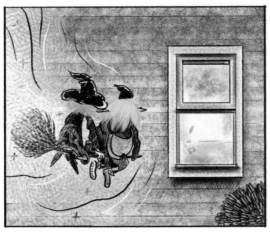

Thanks for your help, Dearie.

What, uh ... Where ...

Uh ...? How did we ...?

Thank you for taking me trick-or-treating!

Right, trick-or-treating. *That's* where we were.

Er, right ... and now it's late. Time for bed, *young lady.*

Yes, Mom. I'm **really** tired.

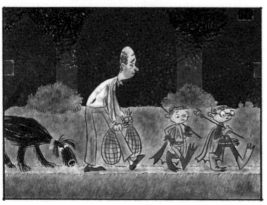

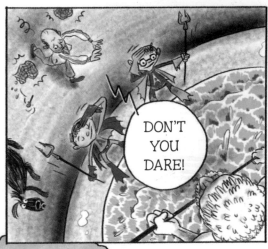

TWEEEEEEEET!

OUT!

NOW!

IS *THIS* WHAT YOU TEACH YOUR CHILDREN?

But —

Dad would like to
go home now.

But —

HOT BATH! **NOW!**

SOON ...

mrphles?

BUBBLES!

NO! NO, NO, NO.

I'VE HAD ENOUGH **AQUA-HEROES** FOR ONE NIGHT.

ANTHONY?

Now behave. Both of you. I'll be sitting *right here!*

nod

nod

SHAKE

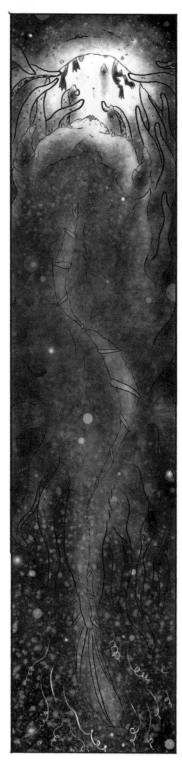

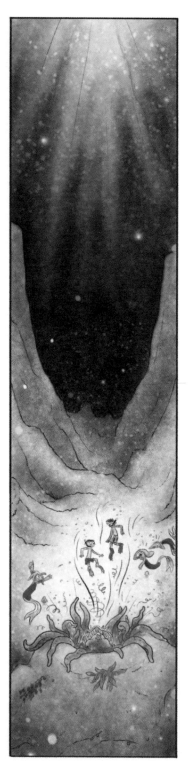

pant
pant
pant

PHOO

ZZZ...

44

Hi, Gemma. I'll be there in three.

'kay, Hiroko.

Hi, Malaya. We'll be there in four.

'kay, Gemma.

50

A *NURSE?* A *FAIRY?* GIVE ME A **BREAK!**

A BALLERINA AND A MERMAID? *THAT IS SO LAME!*

53

LET'S DO IT AGAIN!

clop
clop clop clop

doonk

splat   *splut*

Oops!

Eek!

trip

EWWW, GROSS!

THAT LAST KID WAS *TOO* SCARED.

HEY, LOOK! IT'S THOSE BOYS WHO CALLED US *LAME.*

LET'S SHOW THEM!

AIIIEEEE!

YIKES

HELP

RAR!

NICE TO SEE YOU AGAIN! DON'T BE A STRANGER!

HEH HEH HEH HEH HEH

THAT WAS A *PRETTY GOOD* SCARE.

Yeah, good scare. *HEH HEH HEH.*

WHO ARE YOU?

NONE OF YOUR BUS —

OW!

We've just moved here. I'm Drachel.

smak!

Buffy.

MY NAME IS STELLAMOON.

And miss manners here is called **Slurp.**

Yeah, manners! *HEH HEH HEH.*

WE TRAVEL MUCH. WE DON'T STAY LONG.

OH, TO HAVE A HOME WHERE WE BELONG.

Aw!

What *dingbat* is trying to say is that we live there, next door, and we're having a party. *Wanna come?*

A **HALLOWEEN** PARTY? WITH FOOD AND DRINKS?

YEAH, SURE, A *HALLOWEEN* PARTY.

With **LOTS** of drinks. *HEH HEH HEH.*

I don't remember ever seeing this place before.

AWESOME
DECORATIONS!

COME ON,
THE PARTY
IS UP HERE.

ZIP!

WOULD YOU
LIKE TO SEE
MY ROOM?

THE PARTY IS IN HERE!

THIS ISN'T A *PARTY!* THERE'S NO *MUSIC.* THERE'S *NO FOOD.* THERE'S *NOTHING* TO DRINK!

It's true. We have no music and we have no food.

BUT DRINKS WE SURE DO HAVE.

OH, *REALLY?*

WHERE *ARE* THEY?

WELL, THE DRINKS WOULD BE ...

... YOU!

MEANWHILE DOWNSTAIRS ...

Don't you have a place to sleep?

THIS IS WHERE I SLEEP.

Ohhhh.

MEANWHILE DOWNSTAIRS ...

Do you get to stay up late?

ALL THE TIME.

WOW. YOU'RE *SO* LUCKY.

DO YOU HAVE TO GET UP EARLY?

ALL THE TIME.

WOW. YOU'RE SO LUCKY!

THE DOOR WON'T *OPEN!*

YOUNG LADIES!

I DON'T EVEN LIKE BLOOD, DO YOU?

No, me neither! It makes me want to faint.

IT GIVES ME THE HICCUPS!

Stella *dahlink*, time to say good-bye to your guest.

I'M SURE YOUR PARENTS VOULD NOT BE PLEASED. NEXT TIME CALL FIRST TO MAKE A **PLAY DATE.**

creeak

CLICK

I had fun tonight. Let's do this again!

ONE NIGHT ...

BUT NOT JUST ANY NIGHT ...

SOMETHING HAPPENED.

IT HAPPENED HERE ...

AND IT HAPPENED HERE ...

AND IT EVEN HAPPENED HERE.

WELCOME

S'LAM

NO ONE DARES TO TALK ABOUT IT ...

BUT EVERYONE REMEMBERS ...

Dear Diary
Tonight has been an absolute nightmare, and I don't mean that in a good way

THAT ONE *SPOOKY NIGHT.*

For Dad, who once made me the coolest astronaut costume ever — D.B.
Thank you forever to Cailin. For my little monsters, Susanna and Oscar — D.H.

Text © 2012 Dan Bar-el
Illustrations © 2012 David Huyck

Kids Can Press acknowledges the financial support of the Government of Ontario, through the
Ontario Media Development Corporation's Ontario Book Initiative; the Ontario Arts Council; the
Canada Council for the Arts; and the Government of Canada, through the BPIDP, for our publishing
activity.

Published in Canada by
Kids Can Press Ltd.
25 Dockside Drive
Toronto, ON M5A 0B5

Published in the U.S. by
Kids Can Press Ltd.
2250 Military Road
Tonawanda, NY 14150

www.kidscanpress.com

Edited by Tara Walker and Karen Li
Designed by David Huyck and Rachel Di Salle

The hardcover edition of this book is smyth sewn casebound.
The paperback edition of this book is limp sewn with a drawn-on cover.
Manufactured in Shen Zhen, Guang Dong, P.R. China, in 5/2012 by Printplus Limited

CM 12 0 9 8 7 6 5 4 3 2 1
CM PA 12 0 9 8 7 6 5 4 3 2 1

Library and Archives Canada Cataloguing in Publication

Bar-el, Dan
          That one spooky night / written by Dan Bar-el ; illustrated by David Huyck.

ISBN 978-1-55453-751-8 (bound) ISBN 978-1-55453-752-5 (pbk.)

1. Graphic novels. I. Huyck, David, 1976– II. Title.

PN6733.B37T43 2012   j741.5'971   C2012-901589-X

Kids Can Press is a /corus™ Entertainment company